Nothing
But the
Marvelous

Nothing But the Marvelous

(Expanded)

Wisdoms of Henry Miller

Edited by

Blair Fielding

CAPRA PRESS
SANTA BARBARA

Special thanks to Caroline Roberts
and to Valentine Miller

Cover and book design by Frank Goad, Santa Barbara
Editorial assistance by David Dahl
Printed by McNaughton & Gunn

Library of Congress Cataloguing-in-Publication Data

Miller, Henry, 1891-1980
Nothing but the marvelous (expanded) : wisdoms of
Henry Miller / Blair Fielding, editor.
p. cm.
ISBN 0-88496-440-X (alk. paper)
1. Miller, Henry, 1891——Quotations. 2. Quotations,
American. I. Title. II. Fielding, Blair

PS3525.I5454 A6 1999
818'.5202 21 —dc21

Capra Press
P.O. Box 2068
Santa Barbara, CA 93120

Nothing But the Marvelous

What were the subjects which formed my style, my character, my approach to life. Broadly these: The love of life itself, the pursuit of truth, wisdom and understanding, mystery, the power of language, the antiquity and the glory of man, eternality, the purpose of existence, the oneness of everything, self-liberation, the brotherhood of man, the meaning of love, the relation of sex to love, the enjoyment of sex, humor, oddities, and eccentricities in all life's aspects, travel, adventure, discovery, prophecy, magic (white and black), art, games, confessions, revelations, mysticism, more particularly the mystics themselves, the varieties of faith and worship, the marvelous in all realms and under all aspects, for there is only the marvelous and nothing but the marvelous.

The Books in My Life

Foreword

Henry Miller became my friend and soulmate. He made me aware of the reality of my inner being and the need to listen to it. While his name has been synonymous with censorship and scandal, it has been equally equated with creativity, wisdom and liberation.

Tropic of Cancer was my introduction to his writing, a book I first found shocking in its explicit language and sexuality. Yet through the maze of my own moral and feminist values, I experienced Miller's incredible honesty and openness. I was left with the vision of a man on a passionate journey for truth and freedom who inspired me to embark on my own journey.

Now, through this expanded edition of *Nothing But The Marvelous*, I again share some of Miller's wisdoms that have meant so much to me over the years.

—BLAIR FIELDING

Henry Miller
THE MAN

AGE

Perhaps the most comforting thing about growing old gracefully is the increasing ability not to take things too seriously.

Sextet

When I was young, I would be exultant one day and depressed the next. In later life from the middle forties on, I was on a more serene level.

My Life and Times

If at eighty you're not a cripple or an invalid, if you have your health, if you still enjoy a good walk, a good meal (with all the trimmings), if you can sleep without first taking a pill, if birds and flowers, mountains and sea still inspire you, you are a most fortunate individual and you should get down on your knees morning and night and thank the good Lord for his savin' and keepin' power. If you are young in years but already weary in spirit, already on the way to becoming an automaton, it may do you good to say to your boss—under your breath, of course—"Fuck you, Jack! You don't own me." If you can whistle up your ass, if you can be turned on by a fetching bottom or a lovely pair of teats, if you can

fall in love again and again, if you can forgive your parents for the crime of bringing
you into the world, if you are content to get
nowhere, just take each day as it comes, if
you can forgive as well as forget, if you can
keep from growing sour, surly, bitter and
cynical, man you've got it half licked.

Sextet

AMERICA

It seems as if we were conceived in violence
and hatred, as if we were born to plunder,
rape and murder. Our history books gloss
over the cruelties and abominations, the
immoral behavior of our leaders, the fact, to
take a small example, that one of the greatest men we produced, Thomas Jefferson,
had illegitimate children by a Negro slave of
his. They were nearly all slave holders, these
men who formed this great democracy of
ours. They named it a republic and a democracy, but it never *was* and is not even one
now. A few patrician, wealthy families control the government of these states.

Four Visions of America

When Lincoln issued the Emancipation
Proclamation we thought we had put an end
to slavery. We never imagined the Northern

ghettos, with racial problems far worse than the South ever knew. In addition to black slaves we created *white* slaves—the slaves of the machine age. The Ku Klux Klan still exists. The Mafia also exists! We may not have pogroms but anti-Semitism flourishes just as strongly as ever.

Indeed, for all our talk of progress, we are just as narrow-minded, prejudiced, bloody-thirsty as ever we were. Just to look at the military situation—the Pentagon!—is enough to give one the shivers. The last war—Vietnam—what foul doings! Tamerlane and Attila are nothing compared to our latter-day monsters armed with nuclear weapons, napalm, etc. If Hitler subsidized genocide, what about *us*? We have been practicing genocide from our very inception! Whoever disagrees with us, away with him! That goes for Indian, Negro, Mexican, anyone. And then there is the TV and the cinema. With them everything goes. Children grow up watching crime, watching murder, thievery, torture, everything imaginable that is foul, retarded, barbarous. All part of our beloved "progress." And we wonder why, as a nation, as a people, we are falling apart.

Four Visions of America

Just as one "pays one's dues" to become a movie star, as they say, so a bold, fearless writer pays in one way or another. I paid by going hungry, by being censored, by waiting until I was sixty years old before I could open a bank account. The fact that under Hitler I might have been tortured and shot doesn't sweeten the pill. In a sense, censorship is with us always. The men in power know how to protect themselves. The man who got away with it, as I said earlier, was Nixon. And, to be honest, I see nothing to prevent another Nixon from arising tomorrow. We have not improved; politics is still the same dirty game it always was. Worst of all, or so it would seem, human beings don't change. A thousand Billy Grahams wouldn't alter things by a hair. Among occultists there seems to be a belief that if ever a fundamental change for the better occurs, it will be in America. I would like nothing better than for this to become the truth. Bitter and unpalatable as my words may sound, I do not hate America or even Americans. If I look upon our history as a total flop, I could say the same about most civilized countries. As I said somewhere I can think of no individual in any of the great countries of the world who can say, as do the Pygmies: "We are content as we are. We see no reason to change!" Indeed the very thought is unthinkable to civilized man. And of all the civilized peoples in the world I regard the American as the most restless, the most unsatisfied, the idiot who thinks he can change the world into his own image of it. In the process of making the world better, as he foolishly imagines, he is poisoning it, destroying it. Walt Whitman observed the process taking place over a hundred years ago. He referred to us as a nation of lunatics. Walt Whitman may well have been the greatest American who ever lived!

Four Visions of America

Sometimes, in traveling about Greece, in listening to the tales of Greeks who have worked in the mines in Arizona, Montana, Alaska, men from the lumber camps, the farms, the steel mills, the automobile factories, men who ran fruit stands or restaurants or soda water fountains, florists from Washington Heights or Cathedral Parkway, sometimes in listening to their fervid praise of America, I begin to wonder if I am not wrong about my own country. Another thought often occurs to me, in moments of loneliness, when the barriers of race and language isolate me from those about me— the thought that in a vastly diminished way

I am being privileged to experience the emotions of the countless immigrants who have come to America to make a home, to know some pale reflection of their struggles, their need for comradeship, for a wee touch of human sympathy. I try to think what my life might be if I were obliged to remain in a foreign country, to earn my living there, to learn the language, to adapt myself to their ways. The few Americans who have changed their nationality have done so under entirely different circumstances than the immigrant whom we receive. For an American it is a luxury, a grotesque whim which he is pleased to indulge. It is never an act of necessity, of despair or desperation. Once an American always one.

Sextet

America tries to give to the world an image of a unified nation, "one and indivisible." Nothing could be farther from the truth. We are a people torn with strife, divided in many ways, not only regionally. Our population contains some of the poorest and most neglected people in the world. It probably also contains the most rich people of any country in the world. There is race prejudice to a great degree and inhumanity to man even among the dominant Caucasians.

As I hinted earlier, America is rapidly going down the drain. … We Americans may one day reach all the planets and bring back from each small quantities of soil, but, we will never reach the heart of the universe, which resides in the soul of even the poorest, the lowliest of human creatures.

I am afraid that the old adage, "Brothers under the skin," is no longer true, if ever it were. The Western nations are not to be trusted, no matter how democratic their governments may become. As long as the rich rule there will be chaos, wars, revolutions. The leaders to look to are not in evidence. One has to hunt them out. One should remember, as Swami Vivekananda once put it, that "before Gautama there were twenty-four other Buddhas."

Today we can no longer look for saviours. Every man must look to himself. As some great sage once said: "Don't look for miracles, you are the miracle."

Sextet

BEHAVIOR

Given only half a chance, men will express the best that is in them.

The World of Sex

The crisis through which we are going... is rooted in the fact that we all hold beliefs contrary to our behavior.

Remember to Remember

Why is it that the thousand and one figures of the earth—laborer, artisan, actor, dancer, poet, drunkard, courtesan, musician— depicted by the Japanese masters seem near and dear to us, whereas similar themes by our native artists leave us cold? What is lacking in our everyday figures, our native scenes? Why do they inspire dread, ridicule, or disgust? Is it because there is no longer any relation between what a man is and what he does, what he believes and how he acts?

The Paintings of Henry Miller:
Paint As You Like and Die Happy

To dream a new world is to live it daily, each thought, each glance, each step, each gesture killing and recreating, death always a step in advance. One should act as if the next step were the last, *which it is.*

Hamlet Letters

CONTENTMENT

Though it may seem irrelevant, I feel impelled at this juncture to put in a word or two about the Pygmies. I remember with what surprise and elation I read one day about these strange people. The book was by a man who had lived with them and seemingly knew whereof he spoke. I got the impression that these little people of the forest knew nothing of ambition, had no desire to leave their habitat (the forest), prayed to no god, carried no baggage, had no history, and were perfectly content to live day by day—but above all, that they displayed no interest in bettering their condition. If they came to a rushing stream and had to build a bridge in order to cross it, they did so as a matter of course. They built it and moved on; but first they enjoyed their work, that is to say, before moving on they ran back and forth over it, played with it, as it were. They built the same kind of bridge every time, as had their forbears for thousands of years. They didn't try to make a better bridge each time. Nor did they dream of leaving their home, the forest, and taking up a more stable kind of life. They were content not only with their surroundings but with their life. They lived as they had always lived. *Why change?*

Yes, *why change?* I asked myself. How wonderful to accept life on its own terms! How wonderful to accept one's own self! *Improvement.* . . . I doubt that the word exists in their vocabulary. And though it does exist in ours, it is difficult to see what of value has been accomplished through endless improvement. Certainly the civilized man does not yield the image of contentment, either with himself or with his surroundings; nor is he more peaceable, more loving, more kindhearted, than these little "savages" who dwell in the forest.

The Paintings of Henry Miller:
Paint As You Like and Die Happy

CULTURE

Most people are born blind, deaf and mute. They think that acquiring what is called "Culture" will restore these missing faculties. They learn to recite names—of authors, composers, actors, and so on. They pass these off for the real thing. Lectures, for example, are most important to them: the easy way to imbibe culture. I have always been leery of Culture.

Book of Friends: A Trilogy

DEATH

They are dying miserably, here in America, though they have forked out the most exorbitant sums to doctor, surgeon and hospital.

They may be given wonderful funerals, but no one has yet succeeded in making them die peacefully, nobly, serenely. Few enjoy the luxury of dying in their own beds.

Big Sur and the Oranges
of Hieronymous Bosch

I believe that within the next hundred years people will die blissfully, without suffering, without fear. The more fully we embrace our lives, live our lives, the easier it is to accept the notion of death. Yet, it's the physical suffering that is the most frightening thing about dying I feel. With all our scientific knowledge you'd think we would've solved that one long ago.

Reflections

...that's the only death, that's the real death. Not this death when you depart the body, but being dead while you are alive, that's the real death.

This is Henry, Henry Miller from Brooklyn

DESIRE

The frantic desire to live, to live at any cost, is not a result of the life rhythm in us, but of the death rhythm.

Henry Miller on Writing

As we drag along we carry with us dead images of live moments in the past. Until the day we meet—her. Suddenly the world is no longer the same. Everything has altered. But how can the world be altered in the wink of an eye? It is an experience we all know, yet it brings us no closer to truth. We go on knocking at the door.

The World of Sex

CHARACTER

In the end you have to come back to yourself. It has got to be *you* doing something, whatever you decide upon. Do what you think you have to do and don't try to follow somebody else's pattern because he was successful. You can't be that way. You are you. You're absolutely unique and each one has his own destiny. We can learn as much as we wish, listen to the greatest masters and so on, but what we do, what we become, is determined by our character.

It is possible to transmute the bad into the good, the wrong into the right. There is always this possibility. It would be an utterly uninteresting world if everything remained what it seems to be. I do believe in transmutation. For example, two men are put in prison. One man is utterly despairing; if released he may commit murder again. The other man goes through some inner change and comes out a new man.

My Life and Times

EDUCATION

Usually what is taught in school must be unlearned. Life is the teacher.

The Paintings of Henry Miller:
Paint As You Like and Die Happy

What is called education is to me utter nonsense and detrimental to growth. Despite all the social and political upheavals we have been through the authorized educational methods throughout the civilized world remain, in my mind at least, archaic and stultifying. They help to perpetuate the ills which cripple us.

Sextet

We are not educating our children to be heroes or saints; we are making robots of them.

Gliding Into The Everglades

The more we advance in knowledge the more stunted and crippled we become as individuals.

Gliding Into The Everglades

The job of discovering things for yourself is far better than learning it in school. That's why I am against schools in general.

I tried not to send my children to school when I was in Big Sur but the authorities would not permit it. I believe all schools are destructive. They kill curiosity and the desire to learn.

My Life and Times

EUTHANASIA

If we cannot better the conditions under which we live we can at least offer an immediate and painless way out. There is the escape through euthanasia. Why is it not offered the hopeless, miserable millions for whom there is no possible chance of enjoying even a dog's life? We were not asked to be born; why should we be refused the privilege of making our exit when things become unbearable? Must we wait for the atom bomb to finish us off all together?

Sextet

EVIL

The evil is in us, in our dissatisfaction with the condition of life we find ourselves in.

The Paris Review

FOOD

I don't believe in health foods and diets. I have probably been eating the wrong things all my life—and have thrived on it. I eat to enjoy food. What I do I do first for enjoyment.

On Turning Eighty

What I do eat I eat with gusto and relish. It nourishes my spirit if not my body. The highest moments of my life have always been around the table when the food was good, the wine plentiful and good, and the talk ran high.

Conversation with Ben Grauer

FRIENDSHIP

...a life without friends is no life, however, snug and secure it may be.

Book of Friends: A Trilogy

A true friend is one who picks up right where you left off, whether it's been a week, a month or twenty years.

Reflections

When I say friends, I mean friends. Not everybody can be your friend. It must be someone as close to you as your skin, someone who imparts color, drama, meaning to your life, however snug and secure it may be.

Book of Friends: A Trilogy

...there is an absolute, and that must be in the heart. We must all meet, everyone who has something in common with another, in this domain where there is absolute trust, confidence, loyalty, integrity. If not, everything crumbles away.

A Literate Passion

It's been my good fortune always to have two or three good friends I could count on in time of need. To be blessed with just *one* good friend is usually sufficient. Friends more than made up (for me) the absence of money. And when I say friends I mean ordinary individuals, not exceptional ones. But they were exceptional in their ability to give, to serve, to be at one's beck and call. Nearly always these friends possessed a good sense of humor. They were never preachers or advisers. In fact there was always something a bit dotty or eccentric about them. One might say clownlike, I suppose. Above all, they were always unselfish.

Book of Friends: A Trilogy

What most people fear when they think of

old age is the inability to make new friends. If one ever had the faculty of making friends one never loses it however old one grows. Next to love, friendship, in my opinion, is the most valuable thing life has to offer.

Sextet

GOVERNMENT

It's the imbeciles who run the world. It would be better to put simpletons in the legislature than today's lot of rats and vermin! Imagine a world governed by a trio like Chaplin, Satchmo and Picasso. Even in the after-life they can do more for us than the men in control at present!

I'm No Worse Than The Next
(J'suis Pas Plus Con Qu'un Autre)

I feel the world should be run by women. It would be the kind of a world—one world— I have often dreamed about. Would any man, woman, or child ever go hungry at the hands of say, a Jewish stateswoman?

Reflections

As for freedom of thought, freedom to express one's ideas—not to speak of living them out—where is the government which ever permitted this? Conformity is the rule, and conformity will be the rule as long as men believe in governing one another.

Remember to Remember

The real revolution is taking place constantly. And the name for this deeper process is emancipation—self-liberation in other words. There can only be government—that is, abdication of the self, of one's own inalienable rights—where there are incomplete beings. The New Jerusalem can only be made of and by emancipated individuals.

The Books in My Life

HERO

And what is the hero? Primarily one who has conquered his fears. One can be a hero in any realm; we never fail to recognize him when he appears. His singular virtue is that he has become one with life, one with himself. Having ceased to doubt and question, he quickens the flow and the rhythm of life. The coward, per contra, seeks to arrest life's flow. He arrests nothing, to be sure, unless it be himself. Life moves on, whether we act as cowards or as heroes. Life has no other discipline to impose, if we would but realize it, than to accept life unquestioningly. Everything we shut our eyes to, everything we run away from, everything we deny, denigrate or despise, serves to defeat us in the end. What seems nasty, painful, evil can become a source of beauty, joy and strength, if faced with open mind. Every moment is a golden one for him who has the vision to recognize it as such.

The World of Sex

The celebrated biographies give us the sufferings and hardships of the great. But the sufferings and hardships of the unknown are often more eloquent. The tribulations of fate weave a mantle of unsuspected heroism about these lesser figures. To win through sheer force of genius is one thing; to survive and continue to create when every last door is slammed in one's face is another. Nobody acquires genius: it is God given. But one *can* acquire patience, fortitude, wisdom, understanding. Perhaps the greatest gift the little men have to offer us is this ability to accept the conditions which life imposes, accept one's own limitations, in other words. Or, to put it another way—to love what one does whether it causes a stir or not. Of the highest men Vivekananda once said: "They make no stir in the world. They are calm, silent, unknown."

The Paintings of Henry Miller: Paint As You Like and Die Happy

HOPE

The hope that we may one day awaken to a condition of life utterly different from that which we experience daily makes men willing victims of every form of tyranny and suppression. Man is stultified by hope and fear.

The Books in My Life

Hope is a bad thing. It means that you are not what you want to be. It means that part of you is dead, if not all of you. It means that you entertain illusions. It's a sort of spiritual clap I should say.

The Cosmological Eye

HUMANITY

I'm thinking the only solution for *homo sapiens* is to die out. Another kind of human being has to come into existence. And he has to have a different consciousness. He won't have these problems of ours. He'll have others. He won't have what I call miserable, petty problems. The lowest problems to me are hunger, war, injustice. These are problems we should have solved eons ago.

My Life and Times

If we could all go on strike and honestly dis-
avow all interest in what our neighbor is
doing we might get a new lease on life. This
is a pipe dream I know. People only go on
strike for better working conditions, better
wages, better opportunities to become something other than they are.

The Colossus of Maroussi

Let a man believe in himself and he will find
a way to exist despite the barriers and tradi-
tions which hem him in.

Stand Still Like the Hummingbird

IDEALISM

I notice that the desire to reform moves man
away from his neighbor, and not towards
him. It leads to isolation. To concern for the
self. When one has grown utterly weary of
trying to aid men one returns to the flock
and then one really aids, just by his presence, because then the sum of experiences,
of suffering, of self-analysis and soul-strug-
gle have mellowed the individual and he
can aid because he speaks and moves out of
a ripe, conscious wisdom—not through pre-
cepts, ideas, formulas. I'm thinking that perhaps the root of all dissension between
"friends" is the quality of idealism con-

tained in it. It is again a too sacred, too private, too isolated thing. Pure love, pure friendship—these are ideals. These may exist now and then, and they are beautiful things to behold. But they are not goals. They are phenomenal and accidental.

A Literate Passion

INERTIA

Very, very few Americans enjoy the work they are obliged to perform day in and day out. The vast majority are condemned, just as much as any slave, any convict, any halfwit. Who really loves what he is doing day in and day out? What holds one to job, trade, profession or pursuit? Inertia.

*Big Sur and the
Oranges of Hieronymous Bosch*

In the midst of one's work, in the midst of the best intentions, in the midst of doing good for the world, or making the world happy, etc., one begins to have the gravest doubts. One has to find out whether one is acting because he wishes to do good or bring happiness or spread truth, etc. or whether it is out of egotism or compulsion or auto-therapy that one is acting. In other words, the ground gives way under your feet. That is where I am. That is why I give way to inertia. I'd rather not act than act for false reasons.

A Literate Passion

LAUGHTER

It should be borne in mind that although my heart was breaking, I could still enjoy a good laugh. It was this ability to laugh in spite of everything that saved me. I had already known that famous line from Rabelais—"For all your ills I give you laughter." I can say from personal experience that it is a piece of the highest wisdom. There is so precious little of it today—it's no wonder the drug pushers and the psychoanalysts are in the saddle.

Book of Friends: A Trilogy

I know it is difficult to preserve a sense of humor in a world which produces atom bombs like vegetables. But if we had a stronger sense of humor perhaps there would be no need to resort to that dolorous experiment of self-defense by mutual extinction.

Sextet

LIFE

When you are convinced all the exits are blocked, either you take to believing in miracles or you stand still like the hummingbird. The miracle is that the honey is always there, right under your nose, only you were too busy searching elsewhere to realize it. The worst is not death but being blind, blind to the fact that everything about life is in the nature of the miraculous.

Stand Still Like the Hummingbird

To lead a life divorced from books and the making of books, to live without sex, without human companionship, is it so dreadful? Even a writer can do it, if he knows how to live with himself. That is what I mean: I have learned to live with myself and like it.

The World of Sex

But I am not a saint, and probably never will be one. Though it occurs to me, as I make this assertion, that I have been called that more than once, and by individuals whom the court would never suspect capable of holding such an opinion. No, I am not a saint, thank heavens! Nor even a propagandist of a new order. I am simply a man, a man born to write, who has taken as his theme the story of his life. A man who has made it clear, in the telling, that it was a good life, a rich life, a merry life, despite the ups and downs, despite the barriers and obstacles (many of his own making), despite the handicaps imposed by stupid codes and conventions. Indeed, I hope that I have made more than that clear, because whatever I may say about my own life which is only a life, is merely a means of talking about life itself, and what I have tried, desperately sometimes, to make clear is this, that I look upon life itself as good, good no matter on what terms, that I believe it is we who make it unlivable, we, not the gods, not fate, not circumstances.

Letter from Henry Miller to Trygve Hirsch

One can know and accept the reality of death without pretending at the same time to understand it. The wise man knows that life too is beyond his understanding; but he knows what life is and he can accept it.

Hamlet Letters

So, whether the world is going to pieces or not, whether you are on the side of the angels or the devil himself, take life for what it is, have fun, spread joy and confusion.

Sextet

MATERIALISM

We grumble and complain when we suffer minor losses, minor setbacks. From the standpoint of the soul, privation and deprivation are important elements in the building of character.

As a nation we are regarded as a people living in luxury. We have only to think of the comparison between a half-naked guru somewhere in Asia and one of the millions of hardhats (without brains) who ride around in expensive cars and earn wages which, in the eyes of a poverty-stricken Hindu, are comparable to the bounty of a rajah.

Naturally, in the make-up of these well-paid American workers there is not an ounce of soul.

Gliding Into The Everglades

What I am trying to say perhaps is that there was a light touch to things in the old days, more affection, more warmth, more devotion and loyalty. Advertising was only in its infancy. The public relations man was unknown.

Book of Friends: A Trilogy

In two short centuries we are practically going down the drain. *Ausgespielt!* No one is going to mourn our passing, not even those we helped to survive. In the brief span of our history we managed to poison the world. We poisoned it with our ideas of progress, efficiency, mechanization. We made robots of our stalwart pioneers. We dehumanized the world we live in.

Four Visions of America

MEN

Men are the worst babies when it comes to love. Especially American men who have the worst time of all surrendering their precious egos. Because love implies a giving up of sorts, vulnerability, loss of power in one sense, the sense of self, of ego. Man does not recognize what a gem he has in woman and that through the experience of truly loving her, of giving himself up to her, he learns his greatest lessons in life.

Reflections

Though I have nothing to say in defense of the Western man, the so-called "civilized man", I do think that the Japanese man has still a lot of the barbarian in him. His politeness is mock politeness. He is at bottom insensitive, egotistical, brutal. How this same breed of man could create an art and a literature of such poignancy is just as mysterious as the work of his counterpart, the Western man. Both have been committed, from time immemorial, to war, rape, plunder and destruction. They have glorified women in their arts but treated them like dirt in everyday life.

Gliding Into The Everglades

What prevents the Japanese woman from rebelling? That ridiculous thing called tradition or brute male force? But, just as those tiny, backward oil countries are getting a strangle-hold on America, the supposed giant, so the Japanese woman could easily make a ninny of her Japanese man. There are a hundred different ways to go about it. Unfortunately, I doubt that she can find it in her heart to do this to her Japanese man. She is a creature of love, she needs his love, whether he be a tyrant, a blood sucker or a pimp. It may take her another thousand years before she discovers that all she is receiving is counterfeit love. It is not only her tragedy but the tragedy of women the world over. What makes it so deplorable, so cruel and so unwarranted in her case is that she was made for greater, nobler things. One is almost tempted to say she must be stupid. But if she is, her men are a thousand times more stupid.

Women are where they are today because men rule the roost. And, at bottom, men are weaklings. Despite their ability to make war, to massacre, rape, plunder, they are idiots. Fortunately they are bringing about their own destruction. Soon our civilization will be finished, the earth itself will be finished, history will be at an end. ...

The world men have created is a disgrace, an insult to the Creator. Man is an idiot, a rank idiot.

Gliding Into The Everglades

MUSIC

In the end I think of music as a saving grace for all humanity. As the universal language it transcends the boundaries of nationality, social strata, and political ideology. Whether we are educated or uneducated, rich or poor, whether we speak the same tongue or not, we still possess the ability to communicate our feelings to one another through music. The world would be a terrible place without it, a miserable place.

Reflections

NONSENSE

Above everything, to the man of today life seems to have no meaning. It is often said that the prime phenomenon, or state of mind, is that of wonder. This too he has obviously lost. We try to explain the universe in terms of scientific theories, but we are unable to explain even the simplest phenomena. We overlook the fact that meaning comes only when we discover the purposelessness of creation. We mistake order and classification for explanation. We cannot abide the notion of disorder or chaos, yet the need for such an admission is essential. Likewise the need for utter nonsense. Only the genius seems to understand and appreciate the joy of sheer nonsense. Nonsense is the antidote to the monotony and emptiness created by our continual striving for order, *our order*, the antidote to our compulsive efforts to find meaning and purpose where there is none.

Sextet

PARENTING

The child is alive with fire, and we, the adults, smother it as best we can. When we cease throwing the wood of ignorance on the fire, it bursts forth again. Experience is an unlearning, an undoing.

Art & Outrage

When my own two youngsters get to plying me with questions I can't answer, as a rule I tell them the truth—I don't know. And if they say "Mommy would know," or "Harrydick knows," or "God knows, doesn't He?" I say, "Fine! You ask him (or her) next time."

I try to convey the idea that ignorance is no sin. I even hint, softly, to be sure, that there are questions which nobody can answer, not even Mommy or Harrydick. I hope in this way to prepare them for the revelation which is sure to come one day that acquiring knowledge is like biting into a cheese which grows bigger with every bite. I also hope to instill the thought that to answer a question oneself is better than having someone answer it for you. Even if it's the wrong answer!

The gulf between knowledge and truth is infinite. Parents talk a lot about truth but seldom bother to deal in it. It's much simpler to dispense ready-made knowledge. More expedient too, for truth demands patience, endless, endless patience. The happiest expedient of all is to bundle kids off to school just as soon as they can stand the strain. There they not only get "learning," which is a crude substitute for knowledge, but discipline.

Big Sur and the
Oranges of Hieronymous Bosch

POLITICS

Here we boast of having a two-party system. In reality it is a system of pure chaos. Other countries are looked down upon because of their "chaotic" state of affairs. Yet, what could be more chaotic than our own? At the head of this chaos sits a man presumably elected by the people. Yet, ironically, to be elected he must be a millionaire. Think of it! Out of all the possible efficient or potentially efficient leaders of 200,000,000 people, we are permitted to choose between only two. One must be a Democrat and the other a Republican. An Independent stands no chance. And only that Democrat or that Republican stands a chance who is a "friend" not of the people but of the vested "interests." Millions of dollars are spent to elect a fool or knave—in any case, a willing puppet. And this is what is styled a democratic form of government. How much better a benevolent dictatorship!

Four Visions of America

We like to think that the political arena is no place for the artist. Nor is it. But the point is that if a truly creative being were to take over the reins we might see the end of politics and the birth of a meaningful chaos.

Gliding Into The Everglades

One has to be a lowbrow, a bit of a murderer, to be a politician, ready and willing to see people sacrificed, slaughtered, for the sake of an idea, whether a good one or a bad one. I mean, those are the ones who flourish.

The Paris Review

I've never had anything to do with politics. In my opinion it is impossible not to be corrupt in that game. They are all tricksters, evil-doers, con-men.

I'm No Worse than the Next
(J'suis Pas Plus Con Qu'un Autre)

POVERTY

When I talk of poverty, I talk about it in two ways. The first is how terrible it is. The other is that it is a saving thing—that if you haven't known poverty, you haven't known life. Everyone should taste it—and, hopefully, get out of it. It's instructive in the art of living.

Chicago Tribune Magazine

PUNISHMENT

Even at that tender age I felt that punishment was criminal. I couldn't understand why people should be punished...I couldn't even understand why God had the right to punish us for our sins. And, of course, as I later realized, God doesn't punish us—we punish ourselves.

The Air-Conditioned Nightmare

RELATIONSHIPS

Man believes that falling in love is the big thing, whereas it is only a can opener, he's got the rest of his life to live with the woman. And it's the woman who knows more about how to preserve a relationship than man does. She lubricates the wheels of the relationship, so to speak. She's the one who keeps everything running smoothly. She's far more practical than man.

Reflections

The ability to be friends with a woman, particularly the woman you love, is to me the greatest achievement.

On Turning Eighty

When I was studying the Japanese language —for a brief period—my teacher translated for me a beautiful letter to her niece by a noble Japanese woman, who was dying. The niece was about to get married. In it she expounded her probably ancient views on the true relationship between husband and wife. To me it seemed the ideal prescription for a happy, lasting marriage. ... The keynote, as I recall it, was surrender (or submission, if you like) on the part of both the husband and the wife.

Submission, surrender—these words are inadequate. It was more—living for and doing for the other. For, after all, when we try to define love, do we not think of it as living for the one we love, a not thinking of self but a complete concentration on the other? And, if wives and husbands were truly to behave thus, would they not be exalting one another, making of him a king and of her a queen?

Gliding Into The Everglades

RESPONSIBILITY

I don't want to be bitter about life—about love and friendship and all the human, emotional entanglements. I've had more than my share of human disappointments, deprivations, disillusionment. I want to love people and life above all; I want to be able to say always, "if you feel bitter or disillusioned, there is something wrong with yourself, not with people, not with life."

A Literate Passion

We forget that we create our fate every day we live. And by fate I mean the woes that beset us, which are merely the effects of causes which are not nearly as mysterious as we pretend. Most of the ills we suffer from are directly traceable to our own behavior. Man need not live in poverty, vice, ignorance, in rivalry and competition. All these conditions are within his province, within his power to alter.

Big Sur and the
Oranges of Hieronymous Bosch

I realized that I alone was responsible for all the misfortune which had befallen me. The day that truth dawned on me—and it came like a flash—the burden of guilt and suffering fell away. What a tremendous relief it was to cease blaming society, or my parents, or my country.

Stand Still Like the Hummingbird

The situation one finds oneself in is always the situation one has created: we are always at the point or place we desired to be.

Hamlet Letters

SECURITY

If I were to have money I might become careless and negligent, believing in a security which does not exist, stressing those values which are illusory and empty. I have no misgivings about the future. In the dark days to come money will be less than ever a protection against evil and suffering.

The Colossus of Maroussi

No matter how knowledgeable, no matter how wise, no matter how prudent and cautious, we all have an Achilles' Heel. Security is not the lot of man. Readiness, alertness, responsiveness—these are the sole defenses against the blows of fate.

Letter from Henry Miller to Trygve Hirsch

SEX

Sex is impersonal, and may or may not be identified with love. Sex can strengthen and deepen love, or work destructively.

The World of Sex

If there is something wrong about our attitude toward sex then there is something wrong about our attitude toward bread, toward money, toward work, toward play, toward everything. How can one enjoy a good sex life if he has a distorted, unhealthy attitude toward other aspects of life?

The World of Sex

It is true I swim in a perpetual sea of sex, but the actual excursions are fairly limited. I think it's more like this—that I'm always ready to love, always hungry to love. I'm talking about love, not just sex. And I don't mind at all saturating my work with it—sex I mean—because I'm not afraid of it and I almost want to stand up and preach about it.

A Literate Passion

I don't think much of [the sexual revolution in America] to be very honest with you. Look, I believe in permissiveness. I believe anything and everything is possible in bed between two people. And that it's nobody's business but theirs. I don't like the way the youngsters have been going about it. Flaunting it. Making a game of it. I've been largely responsible for it, I'm afraid. Because they only read me part way.

Chicago Tribune Magazine

When I was 21 and I heard Emma Goldman, the anarchist, speak about "free love"—that was the expression then—it sounded good to me. Oh, it was more a question of being able to have sexual relations with the person you were in love with. But today, the way I see it, the word love is sort of omitted. They talk a lot about love-ins and love and love, but I don't feel that the unions between couples are based on a great love for one another. It's more like experimentation. I think this complete freedom doesn't make for something interesting. They're bored very quickly.

This is Henry, Henry Miller from Brooklyn

SOCIETY

Focusing on society gets one nowhere. Society is the composite of millions of men living together, millions of separate entities each working out his own salvation, his own creation. There is as much of me in society as there is of society in me. As I change the world changes, imperceptible though it may be. Sounds Emersonian, I know, but no matter. I am convinced to the truth of it. Society is not changing in any haphazard, whimsical manner. Society changes daily according as we change, each and every one of us.

Hamlet Letters

Today I believe that it is possible to be in the world and of it and at the same time beyond it, an attitude which was impossible for me at the age of twenty-one because I did not know the world, because at that time I was intent on *altering* the world, and that in the most ineffective way possible, by a straight-lined, idealistic attitude. Today I am hardly an idealist, nor even a realist, but a confirmed dreamer who accepts the unreal as a solid unshakable fact. Today I believe absolutely that everything about us, our world, our behavior, the skies, the climate, the forms of life, we ourselves, are a creation, that we have the power to create life as we desire it, and that all criticism, all reproach, should be directed against ourselves and ourselves only. Today I assume full responsibility for what I am and where I am.

Hamlet Letters

TABOO

Taboos after all are only hangovers, the product of diseased minds, you might say, of fearsome people who hadn't the courage to live and who under the guise of morality and religion have imposed these things upon us.

The Paris Review

VALUES

We have plenty of money for bombers, sub-marines, warheads, for all that is destructive, but not for culture, not for education, or for relief of the poor. What a thing to say of the supposedly greatest country in the world that thousands of our poor are content to live on dog and cat food. I say thousands, but for all I know it may be millions.

Four Visions of America

I am as guilty as you, my dear Mishima, in trying to make the world a better place to live in. Or at least I began with that hope. In some peculiar way the practise of writing taught me the futility of such a pursuit. Even before I had read St. Francis' words of wisdom I had made the decision to look upon the world with different eyes, to accept it as it is and be content to make my own world. This about face did not blind me to the evils which exist, nor make me indif-ferent to the suffering and misery which men endure. Neither has it made me less critical of the laws, the institutions, the codes of behavior which we continue to live by. It is hard, indeed, for me to imagine a world more absurd, more unreal, than the one we are now living in. It seems, as the

Gnostics of old put it, more like "a cosmic mistake", more like the work of a phony Creator. For the world to become livable there would need to be what Nietzsche called "a transvaluation of values". To put it mildly, it is an insane world in which, alas, the insane are outside the asylum and not inside. In short, so it looks when one would like to have things his own way.

Sextet

We are living in a period which constantly threatens to annihilate not only our personality but our very identity. The extreme prevalence of schizophrenia (now admittedly the disease claiming the greatest number of victims—in America, at least) is but the reflection of the times. We shall not make a new world until we make new men. To the vast majority the thought is terrifying. It means death in the most potent form—death to the present order of men....

Sextet

Jesus said, "consider the lilies of the field, how they grow; they toil not, neither do they spin." The thought behind it is that we are creating this work, not because it has to be done but because we are busybodies and do not know how to swim on the stream of life. We prefer a kind of senseless insect activity to a genuine activity which may often be no activity, plain inaction. I don't say to be quiet, to do nothing. But I say what we do should have sense, should have meaning. And the greater part of what we do every day has damn little meaning.

My Life and Times

VISION

If you have the vision and the urge to undertake great tasks, then you will discover in yourself the virtues and the capabilities required for their accomplishment.

Big Sur and the
Oranges of Hieronymous Bosch

I certainly do not hope to alter the world. Perhaps I can put it best by saying that I hope to alter my own vision of the world. I want to be more and more myself, ridiculous as that may sound.

This is Henry, Henry Miller from Brooklyn

Suddenly I realized how it had been with the struggle to express myself in writing. I saw back to the period when I had the most intense, exalted visions of words written and spoken, but in fact could only mutter brokenly. Today I see that my steadfast desire was alone responsible for whatever progress or mastery I have made. The reality is always there, and it is preceded by vision. And if one keeps looking steadily the vision crystallizes into fact or deed. There is no escaping it. It doesn't matter what route one travels—every route brings you eventually to the goal. "All roads lead to Heaven," is the Chinese proverb. If one accepted that fully, one would get there so much more quickly. One should not be worrying about the degree of "success" obtained by each and every effort, but only concentrate on maintaining the vision, keeping it pure and steady. The rest is sleight-of-hand work in the dark, a genuine automatic process, no less somnambulistic because accompanied by pains and aches.

Sextet

WAR

I have said over and over again that I can understand a man committing murder in passion; if I were a judge I would condone such crimes. But I cannot bring myself to believe that killing indiscriminately in cold blood, which is what war entails, is justifiable. As for killing an idea by killing the man who cherishes it, that to me is simply too preposterous for words.

Remember to Remember

The two superpowers—Russia and the United States, make no bones about their accumulation of weaponry or the sale of it to other nations. One waits breathlessly to see what the Chinese will do, now that they too, have the bomb. The simplest definition I can think of for this so-called civilized behavior is—insanity.

Playboy Magazine

A war is fought for the benefit of the people. By the time the war is over, however, there are no benefits, just debts, death and desolation. All of which has to be paid for.

Remember to Remember

War is only a vast manifestation in dramatic style of the sham, hollow, mock conflicts which take place daily everywhere even in so-called times of peace. Every man contributes his bit to keep the carnage going, even those who seem to be staying aloof.

The Colossus of Maroussi

To return to the other side of the fence, to those who pretend to themselves that peace is a desirable order of things, to those who are always ready to sacrifice their lives for the maintenance of the status quo. The cardplayers are a superb symbol for these individuals. They are old and weary, they have sufficient with which to "get by," they are indifferent to the sufferings of those around them, they ask only to be left alone and in peace. That's the real aspect of the situation today, and even a child can understand it. And even a child, if its mind is not already blunted by education, might understand that the cardplayers are equally guilty before God, that war is brought about through a desire to be left in peace as much as by a desire to expand and conquer.

Hamlet Letters

I believe that the ideal condition for humanity would be to live in a state of peace, in brotherly love, but I must confess I know no way to bring such a condition about. I have accepted the fact, hard as it may be, that human beings are inclined to behave in a way that would make animals blush. The ironic, the tragic thing is that we often behave in ignoble fashion from what we consider the highest motives. The animal makes no excuse for killing his prey; the human animal, on the other hand, can invoke God's blessing when massacring his fellow men. He forgets that

God is not *on* his side but *at* his side.

Sextet

Every time I see a well-trained army marching off to war I think of how those spic and span outfits, those polished boots and polished buttons will look after the first encounter with the enemy. I think of how those millions of bright uniforms are destined to become nothing more than ragged, filthy shrouds covering dead and mutilated bodies. Strange, the importance given the uniform. As if the body were leased for the lifetime of the uniform. When forming your little army I wonder if you ever gave a thought to the possible finish of those uniforms which cost you so much time and effort to pay for.

Sextet

WEAKNESS

But even from a limited, academic, highbound point of view, the traditional art view, how silly it is for critics to be disturbed about slag, excrescences, drift and scoriac. How little they understand the role of the value of the so-called non-essential, the commonplace, the ugly, the inartistic.

Their desire for perfection is so similar to

that false religious attitude which desires only good. You may think I am trying to justify my weakness. No, I am trying to tell you that I learned as much, or more, from the bad, the wrong, the slipshod, the evil, the misfit, and so on, than the other way around. When we speak of a person getting to grips with himself, accepting himself for what he is, we do not simply mean that he admits and recognizes his weaknesses but that he also discovers how important they were in his evolution.

Art & Outrage

Not one of the faithful disciples ever spoke of Jesus farting or even blowing his nose. But he must have, what! Would it have been inartistic, sacrilegious, irreverent to introduce such a note? There are many still who can't excuse him, who refuse to believe, that in his agony on the cross he cried out: "O Lord, why hast thou forsaken me!" A saviour shouldn't have spoken such words, they will tell you. And yet it is this, just this piece of weakness, of doubt, of complaint, that is the most human thing about Jesus, that keeps him linked to us human-all-too-human trash.

Art & Outrage

WISDOM

The wise man, the holy man, the true scholar learns as much from the criminal, the beggar, the whore, as he does from the saint, the teacher, or the Good Book.

The Books in My Life

If only the dead could talk—not about the afterworld but about the one they departed! If only we were able to learn from the experience of others! But we do not learn that way, if indeed we learn at all during our short stay here below. All we can hope to learn is how to live, but for that there are no instructors. Each one has to find out for himself, or as some say, find the Path and become one with it. The irony of it all is that the errors one makes are just as important, or perhaps more important, than the right findings. Trial and error, trial and error—until one gives up trying, which is simply another way of saying gives up butting his head against a stone wall.

Sextet

I maintain that advice is futile. One must find out for himself. It sounds cruel, but it isn't.

My Life and Times

WOMEN

Women have a world all their own. What we men owe to women and why we should adore them and put them in high places is their intuition. That is what men lack.

People Magazine

I have always felt it was woman, not man, who is the stronger sex, the superior one. She has more endurance, she can suffer greater pain, torture, deprivation, and so on. And it is not only her physical stamina that makes her superior. She is in possession of the greatest intelligence there is, one which cannot be measured by men's standards. It has nothing whatever to do with intellectual pursuits or university training. Her intelligence matches that of Mother Nature, it is naturally intuitive, instinctive. She is highly attuned to nature's rhythms and nature's needs. While man struggles to shape the world around him to his needs and to his likings, woman finds a way to harmonize her needs with those of the world in which she lives. Her approach to life is natural, practical, and peace loving while man's is warlike and mechanical.

Reflections

I would value a woman's opinion... who is not prudish or squeamish and who has a critical faculty.

Dear, Dear Brenda

I think the French woman is wonderful because she is the equal of her man and participates in all his activities.

Dear, Dear Brenda

We've had wonderful women, glorious women...who have contributed greatly to the world. Men contributed money and ammunition. I'm against the whole man-made world. Would you believe that I, who have been the sex artist, am against this world that man has created.

People Magazine

Now there are two feminists I admire tremendously, Gloria Steinem and Germaine Greer. I've never met either of them personally but I'm intrigued by them. Both are good looking, feminine, and highly intelligent. Germaine Greer debating with a man makes him look like a pickle. An idiot! I read a fabulous interview with her in Playboy magazine—my God! She was tremendous, forceful, and she didn't have to dress or act like a man in order to make people sit up and take her seriously. It was easy to be responsive to what she was saying because she wasn't attacking, harrassing, or ridiculing. Those are the tactics of men, after all. Her talk was inspirational, eloquent, so articulate you couldn't help but feel moved by her.

Reflections

WORLD

Until we do lose ourselves there can be no hope of finding ourselves. We are of the world, and to enter fully into the world we must first lose ourselves in it. The path to heaven leads through hell, it is said.

The World of Sex

Over many centuries of time a few men have appeared who, to my way of thinking, really understood why the times are permanently bad. They proved, through their own unique way of living, that this sad "fact" is one of man's delusions...if we want to lead a creative life it is absolutely just that we should be responsible for our own destiny.

It is the great mass of mankind, the mob, the people, who create the permanently bad times. The world is only the mirror of ourselves. If it's something to make one puke, why then puke, me lads, it's your own sick mugs you're looking at.

The Cosmological Eye

YOUTH

The whole society from time immemorial has always worshipped youth. Now we all know, who've been through youth, that it isn't such a glorious world. And I don't know how they got all those qualities that they attribute to youth.

Youth is used wrongly, you see. I mean, I think that the young men of 80, see, are the men who could do things. And they have a youth which is the real youth. Do you see what I mean? It isn't a physical youth, it's greater than that—it's a spiritual youth, the youth of the mind and spirit which is eternal.

Los Angles Times Magazine

It was only in my forties that I really began to feel young. By then I was ready for it. ... By this time I had lost many illusions, but fortunately not my enthusiasm, nor the joy of living, nor my unquenchable curiosity.

Sextet

At eighty I believe I am a far more cheerful person than I was at twenty or thirty. I most definitely would not want to be a teen-ager again. Youth may be glorious, but it is also painful to endure. Moreover, what is called youth is not youth, in my opinion; it is rather something like premature old age.

Sextet

Henry Miller
THE ARTIST

ART

Once art is really accepted it will cease to be. It is only a substitute, a symbol-language, for something which can be seized directly. But for that to become possible man must become thoroughly religious, not a believer, but a prime mover, a god in fact and deed.

Henry Miller on Writing

The greatest joy, and the greatest triumph, in art, comes at the moment when, realizing to the fullest your grip over the medium, you deliberately sacrifice it in the hope of discovering a vital hidden truth within you. It comes like a reward for patience—this freedom of mastery which is born of the hardest discipline. Then no matter what you do or say, you are absolutely right and nobody dare criticize you. I sense this very often in looking at Picasso's work. The great freedom and spontaneity he reveals is born, one feels, because of the impact, the pressure, the support of the whole being which, for an endless period, has been subservient to the discipline of the spirit. The most careless gesture is as right, as true, as valid, as the most carefully planned strokes. This I know, and nobody could convince me to the contrary. Picasso here is only demonstrating a wisdom of life which the sage practices on another, higher level.

Sextet

Art includes religion. Art is man, on his way to ordination.

Sextet

THE ARTIST

Going to school gives the illusion that knowledge is what makes an artist. It's like knowing how to write English perfectly. It has very little relation to the art of writing.

My Life and Times

I'm 100 per cent American; I don't deny that. My 10 years in Europe didn't change me. They'd even talk about my speaking French with a Brooklyn accent. But we're such a mercenary people. Faking humility. Arrogant. We don't know—or care—how the other half of the world lives. Also people here don't care about the artist. In Europe, he gets a certain respect just for being one. I'll never forget when I arrived in France with "Writer" on my passport. The customs man extended his hand—"Honored to meet you!" Think of that! Here, my God, you're a writer? You're a bum!

Chicago Tribune Magazine

I don't care who the artist is, if you study him deeply, sincerely, detachedly, you will find that he and his work are one. If it were otherwise the planets would be capable of leaving their orbits.

Art & Outrage

Usually the artist has two lifelong companions, neither of his own choosing. I mean— poverty and loneliness. To have a friend who understands and appreciates your work, one who never lets you down but who becomes more devoted, more reverent, as the years go by, that is a rare experience. It takes only one friend, if he is a man of faith, to work miracles. How distressing it is to hear young painters talking about dealers, shows, newspaper reviews, rich patrons, and so on. All that comes with time—or will never come. But first one must make friends, create them through one's work. What sustains the artist is the look of love in the eyes of the beholder. Not money, not the right connections, not exhibitions, not flattering reviews.

The Paintings of Henry Miller: Paint As You Like and Die Happy

Whoever uses the spirit that is in him creatively is an artist. To make living itself an art, that is the goal.

Big Sur and the
Oranges of Hieronymous Bosch

An artist earns the right to call himself a creator only when he admits to himself that he is but an instrument.

The Time of the Assassins

I nevertheless firmly believe that no world order, no world harmony, is possible until the artist assumes leadership. I mean by this that the artist in man must come to the fore, over against the patriot, the warrior, the diplomat, the fanatical idealist, the misguided revolutionary. It is not against the gods man must rebel—the gods are with him, if he but knew it!—but against his own mediocre, vulgar, blighted spirit. He must free himself to look upon the world as his own divine playground and not as a battlefield of contending egos. He must lift himself by his own bootstraps.

Stand Still Like the Hummingbird

The remarkable thing to observe in children's work is that the child gives the impression of having done it with his whole being. They surrender themselves completely to what is in hand. Whereas even the biggest artist has to wage a constant fight against distraction. He is conscious not only of the future opinions of the critics, the price it will fetch (or not fetch!), the value of his tubes, the nicety of his choice of color or line, but also the temperature of the room, the stains on the floor, the bath he forgot to take, and so on.

Sextet

CENSORSHIP

To put it succinctly and simply as possible, here is my basic attitude toward life, my prayer, in other words. "Let us stop thwarting one another, stop judging and condemning, stop slaughtering one another." I do not implore you to suspend or withhold judgment of me or my work. Neither I nor my work is that important (one cometh, another goeth). What concerns me is the harm you are doing to yourselves. I mean by perpetuating this talk of guilt and punishment, of banning and proscribing, of whitewashing and blackballing, of closing your eyes when convenient, of making scapegoats when there is no other way out. I ask you pointblank—does the pursuance of your limited role enable you to get the most out of life? When you write me off the books, so to speak, will you find your food and wine more palatable, will you sleep better, will you be a better man, a better husband, a better father, than before? These are the things that matter—what happens to you, not what you do to me.

Letter from Henry Miller to Trygve Hirsch

You cannot eliminate an idea by suppressing it, and the idea which is linked with this issue is one of freedom to read what one chooses. Freedom, in other words, to read what is bad for one as well as what is good for one—or, what is simply innocuous. How can you guard against evil, in short, if one does not know what evil is?

But it is not something evil, not something poisonous, which this book *Sexus* offers the Norwegian reader. It is a dose of life which I administered to myself first, and which I not only survived but thrived on. Certainly I would not recommend it to infants, but then neither would I offer a child a bottle of aqua vite. I can say one thing for it unblushingly—compared to the atom bomb, it is full of life-giving qualities.

Letter from Henry Miller to Trygve Hirsch

Rereading the lengthy document today, I am more than ever aware of the absurdity of the whole procedure. (How lucky I am not to be indicted as a "pervert" or "degenerate," but simply as one who makes sex pleasurable and innocent!) Why, it is often asked, when he has so much else to give, did he have to introduce these disturbing, controversial scenes dealing with sex? To answer that properly, one would have to go back to the womb—with or without the analyst's guiding hand. Each one—priest, analyst, barrister, judge—has his own answer, usually a ready-made one. But none go far enough, none are deep enough, inclusive enough. The divine answer, of course is—first remove the mote from your own eye!

Letter from Henry Miller to Trygve Hirsch

I think we all censor ourselves. There are things I could not write. There are certain things I couldn't even say. I think we exercise our own judgment there and we should.

Henry Miller on the Merv Griffin Show

I think that each one can have his own censorship. I know what I don't want to read, but I don't tell others what not to read. The only point about censorship is not to tell other people what to do.

Henry Miller on the Merv Griffin Show

CREATIVITY

To begin is the thing, begin anywhere, any-how. So it goes. What results is not of my bidding. It's either the work of the devil or my guardian angel.

The Paintings of Henry Miller:
Paint As You Like and Die Happy

If only I could believe in work. I hate work. Creation is not work—it's play. But who believes in that? I know it's true, but now it's one of those distant truths—as remote as the stars. It's treasonable even to think this way.

A Literate Passion

We invent nothing, truly. We borrow and recreate. We uncover and discover. All has been given, as the mystics say. We have only to open our eyes and hearts, to become one with that which is.

The Smile at the Foot of the Ladder

We're creators by permission, by grace, as it were. No one creates alone, of and by him-self. An artist is an instrument that registers something already existent, something which belongs to the whole world and which, if he is an artist, he is compelled to give back to the world.

Sexus

I don't have a mind that thinks in a straight line. I explode as I think…in many different directions at once.

My Life and Times

…my quarrel with these analytical individuals is, why can't they accept what they see without trying to explain it? After all, the truest thing one can say about creative work, in whatever field, is that there is an element of magic in it. Pure reason leads nowhere, unless it be to the analyst's couch. The necessity to analyze, to understand, to categorize, answers to some basic need in the onlooker. He cannot rest suspended in thin air. He must know, know the reason why, and in doing so he kills what he sees. How much more interesting and instructive it is to ask a child what he thinks of one's work. Often, after a session with intellectual individuals I feel like saying, "It's *your* problem. Don't ask *me* what it means."

The Paintings of Henry Miller:
Paint As You Like and Die Happy

FAILURE

Sometimes the wrong thing turns out to be the right thing; sometimes a setback is as good, or better, than a push. We seldom realize how much the negative serves to induce the positive, the bad the good.

The Paintings of Henry Miller:
Paint As You Like and Die Happy

And now to the sponge....The sponge is connected with failure. Using the sponge I can sometimes turn a failure into a rather creditable performance. Of course one needs good paper with which to work such magic—a stout, heavy paper of cold press, one that will take much soaking and scrubbing. The trick is to obliterate the original composition as much as possible; then one should turn the paper around and do something absolutely different—*over* what faint trace is left of the original. In this way the background, which was the failure, adds life and interest to the new composition. No one could possibly make such a background deliberately. Somehow the haphazard, meaningless lines of the original failure spark the new composition. There is more than a technical achievement involved in this procedure. What is demonstrated in this wise is what we witness in life itself at times, to wit, the transmutation of bad into good. Making use, in short, of failure itself—using failure as an adjunct to success.

The Paintings of Henry Miller:
Paint As You Like and Die Happy

INSANITY

A good artist must also have a streak of insanity in him, if by insanity is meant an exaggerated inability to adapt. The individual who can adapt to this mad world of today is either a nobody or a sage. In the one case he is immune to art and in the other he is beyond it.

The Paintings of Henry Miller:
Paint As You Like and Die Happy

INSTINCT

More and more I have found that the proper way for me, not for everybody but for me who was not born a painter, had no talent and is still lacking in a great many things, is to follow my instinct, let the brush in my hand decide what I am going to do.

With writing it's the same. I try not to think. I try to uncover whatever is inside me begging to be revealed.

My Life and Times

OBSCENITY

Nothing would be regarded as obscene, I feel, if men were living out their inmost desires.

Remember to Remember

The real nature of the obscene resides in the lust to convert.

Remember to Remember

I've written about 60 books, and only part of them have dealt with obscenity. It was because of my obsession for telling the truth that I fell into this. It was never with the idea of shocking. I don't consider myself as having written pornography. I wrote obscenity, which is pure. But the other thing, pornography, is impure. It's like a caricature of the real thing.

People Magazine

The obscene would be the forthright, and pornography would be the roundabout. I believe in saying the truth, coming out with it cold, shocking if necessary, not disguising it. In other words, obscenity is a cleansing process, whereas pornography only adds to the murk.

The Paris Review

PAINTING

My watercolors are always voyages of adventure and, whether "successful" or unsuccessful, they give me real satisfaction. I can swim in their presence just as gratefully as if they were Picassos or Rembrandts. I am never totally disappointed in them, no matter how bad the attempt.

The Paintings of Henry Miller:
Paint As You Like and Die Happy

People often ask, "If you had your life to live all over again would you do this or that?" Meaning—would you repeat the same mistakes? As for *les amours* I cannot answer, but as for *les aquarelles*, oui! One of the important things I learned in making watercolors was not to worry, not to care too much. I think it was Picasso who said, "Not every picture has to be a masterpiece." Precisely. To paint is the thing. To paint each day. Not to turn out masterpieces. Even the Creator, in making this world, had to learn this lesson. Certainly when he created Man he must have realized that he was in for a prolonged headache.

Sextet

Again I'm painting watercolors, this time not to while away the time or stave off madness but to requite my numerous benefactors for their kindness in sending me little sums of money, clothing, food, umbrellas, painting materials, and so on. Was I to take offense because the generous soul offering me two bucks demanded one of my "good" watercolors? (One of my quondam benefactors had the cheek to ask for a "brace" of watercolors, saying that the two dollars he was transmitting ought to prove ample. I did as he requested, and without a word of sarcasm. After all, how could a lieutenant commander in the United States Navy be expected to know the value of a watercolor?)

The Paintings of Henry Miller:
Paint As You Like and Die Happy

PLAY

Of course, in writing, I think, one writes to discover himself. In this thing [watercolors], I'm just playing—I attach no importance to what I do in painting, not at all. I'm just having a good time. And, I think that this is a very important part of life—that people learn how to play, and that they make life a game, rather than a struggle for goals, don't you know.

This is Henry, Henry Miller from Brooklyn

READING

In a book, for example—I say in a book and not the book, or a certain book—there are lines, just lines, page so and so, top left, that stand out like mountain peaks—and they made you what you have become. No one else but you could respond to those lines. They were written for you. Just as everything else which happens to you was intended for you, and never mistake it.

Art & Outrage

Whoso has the power to affect us more and more deeply each time we read him is indeed a master, no matter what his name, rank or status be.

The Books in My Life

To read is to always interpret.

The Books in My Life

The good reader, like the good author, knows that everything stems from the same source. He knows that he could not participate in the author's private experience were he not composed of the same substance through and through.

The Books in My Life

SUFFERING

Struggle is the most invaluable experience of all. Suffering seems to be the inevitable fate of the creative sensitive types. Poverty, disease, death, unrequited love affairs, and disappointments of every sort fan the flame of the artistic spirit.

The greatest works of art were not created by spoiled brats. They were born for the most part out of a sense of despair, and if not despair then just plain hard work. Somewhere along the line the artist learns the art of transformation; how to celebrate his hungerings and sufferings, turning disappointment into something positive—a great book, a sonata, a film, a painting, or a dance.

Reflections

I have made peace with suffering. Suffering belongs, just as much as laughter, joy, treachery, or what have you. When one perceives its function, its value, its usefulness, one no longer dreads it, this endless suffering which all the world is so eager to dodge.

Stand Still Like the Hummingbird

I wrote all these autobiographical books not because I think myself such an important person but—this will make you laugh—

because I thought when I began that I was telling the story of the most tragic suffering any man had endured. As I got on with it I realized that I was only an amateur at suffering. Certainly I had my full share of it, but I no longer think it was so terrible. That's why I called the trilogy *The Rosy Crucifixion*. I discovered that this suffering was good for me, that it opened the way to a joyous life, through acceptance of the suffering. When a man is crucified, when he dies to himself, the heart opens up like a flower. Of course you don't die, nobody dies, death doesn't exist, you only reach a new level of vision, a new realm of consciousness, a new unknown world. Just as you don't know where you came from, so you don't know where you're going. But that there is something there, before, and after, I firmly believe.

The Paris Review

WRITING

Writing is its own reward.

Hamlet Letters

The difference between me and other writers is that they struggle to get down what they've got up here in the head. I struggle to get out what's below, in the solar plexus, in the nether regions. ˙

> *My Life and Times*

My whole aim in writing has been to tell the truth, as I know it.

> *The Smile at the Foot of the Ladder*

Writing, like life itself, is a voyage of discovery. The adventure is a metaphysical one: it is a way of approaching life indirectly, of acquiring a total rather than a partial view of the universe. The writer lives between the upper and lower worlds: he takes the path in order eventually to become that path himself.

> *Henry Miller on Writing*

What I needed most desperately was a voice with which to express my grief and abandonment. That is how I came to write. My thought was simple and direct. My prayer, I should say, for it virtually took that form. "Give me, O God," is what I kept saying, "the power to express this anguish which afflicts me. Let me tell it to the world, for I can't bear to keep it locked up in my own breast."

> *This is Henry, Henry Miller from Brooklyn*

I said that a writer was a man who had antennae; if he really knew what he was, he would be very humble. He would recognize himself as a man who was possessed of a certain faculty which he was destined to use for the service of others. He has nothing to be proud of, his name means nothing, his ego is nil, he's only an instrument in a long procession.

The Paris Review

To me being a writer was like saying, "I'm going to be a saint, a martyr, a god." It was just as big, just as far away, just as remote as that. For years I only dared dream about it. I didn't even think I had the ability, but it was the one and only thing I wanted to do. Yet to do it I did a thousand other things first.

My Life and Times

When do you begin? How do you start? Most people get frustrated just looking at the blank page. Everybody does. It's the same as looking at a blank canvas. I found a trick that the surrealists discovered, and that was to simply write whatever came to mind—nonsense, no commas, no periods, no sequence of any kind, until what you wanted to say began to come forth. Then you eliminate all the preliminary garbage. I carry on until I grow tired or until I've exhausted what I want to say. But I never let my brain reach the point of exhaustion. I learned a lesson

once. I wrote 45 pages one day and then col-
lapsed. So I always try to keep fresh. It's as
with a reservoir—you never drain it—it takes
too long to fill it up again. Hemingway said
that, I think, but Hemingway was another
one who slaved over his manuscripts and, in
my mind, he did not accomplish too much. I
skim off the surplus, as it were, and the next
day I have something left over to go on with.
That, in general, has been my method of writing. Of course, I get sidetracked very often. I
think I'm going to write about a certain thing
and suddenly another theme will hit me and
I'll go along with it. But the main thing is to
keep the stream alive and flowing. Keep the
flow—that's the primary thought in my head.

My Life and Times

WRITING AND SEX

I've restricted love to sex in my writing. But
I know better than anyone that love may
include sex but it's beyond that.

Conversation with Ben Grauer

The majority of the readers of *Tropic of Cancer* have never read another book of mine,
and they only looked for those pages where
there was sex. That disgusts me.

Full of Life

This women's liberation movement is based on antagonism toward men. In other countries I'm not called a monster. And if you read me thoroughly—the 50 books—you'll know they're not all about sex, and that includes the latest, *Sextet*. Now, they may say, "Well, he's getting old." And there's some truth in that. I don't think about sex all the time. I'm not a monomaniac. But I do think it's a very important part of life, and that it's been mishandled and misunderstand in this country.

Chicago Tribune Magazine

I was telling my adventures you might say. It wasn't the place, therefore, to dwell on love. The sex wasn't too pretty, either. But I played up the scoundrel in myself, don't you know, because he was more interesting than the angel.

Chicago Tribune Magazine

You see, I created a monstrous character in my books and I gave him my name, Henry Miller. He's a demon, a rogue, a scoundrel. He fancies himself the Playboy of the Western World, he thinks he's a great lover, when in reality, he's a shitty lover! He's always too preoccupied with his own needs and desires to open himself up to the woman's needs. It was mostly exaggeration and bravado, you see? That character was me and he wasn't me. It's as if there are two Henry Millers. The one I created, and the one who has survived the best and the worst of his creations.

Reflections

Henry Miller
THE SPIRIT

ACCEPTANCE

Acceptance is the key word. But acceptance is precisely the great stumbling block. It has to be total acceptance and not conformity.
The Time of the Assassins

Perhaps it is a realization of the futility of altering man or things. That ripe speculative attitude which accepts life for what it is, and demands nothing more. Only with full consciousness, not out of inertia, or indifference.
A Literate Passion

I have never regretted anything. Regret, like guilt, is a waste of time.
My Life and Times

I myself do not believe that anything *ought* to happen: what happens is just, I believe. I no longer blame anybody for anything. I accept full responsibility for everything that happens to me, whether it is just or unjust. There are plenty of things which are beyond my control, but what is not beyond my control is my ability to accept or not accept. When the way is easy I forge ahead; when it is too difficult I sit back and let things take their course. There are things I can do and other things I cannot do; I waste no time trying to do the impossible. Nor do I waste energy fighting or hating. I seek to reach my level, that is all. My life is a creation; that others have a part in it I do not deny, but it is my own part of it which interests me and concerns me. There is no "ought" involved; *there is*, that's all. Why do I act? Because I like, because I desire. I do all I can to make my life the way it suits me. The satisfaction is inner, not outer.

Hamlet Letters

ANGELS

The only thing we are missing is angels. In this vast world there is no place for them. And anyway, would our eyes recognize them? Perhaps we are surrounded by angels without knowing it.

I'm No Worse Than The Next
(J'suis Pas Plus Con Qu-un Autre)

The birth of the butterfly is one of the most mysterious and miraculous things in biology. It's a good illustration that, "Out of the ashes rises the Phoenix," or "Out of evil comes good." The butterfly was just a lowly worm in its beginning. The worm didn't live with the moment-to-moment expectation of sprouting wings and taking flight. He lived a useful and productive life, the life of a worm. And he had to die a worm in order to be born as an angel.

Reflections

CHANGE

One's destination is never a place but rather a new way of looking at things.

Big Sur and the
Oranges of Hieronymous Bosch

The world does not change, you change. And how do you change? By different attitudes.

This is Henry, Henry Miller from Brooklyn

St. Francis said, "Don't change the world, change worlds." That's the greatest statement of all because then you leave the world alone. Let it rot. Let it go to hell. But you yourself can create your own world.

People Magazine

COMPLETENESS

When I come into the presence of the serene at heart I am completely myself, thoroughly stilled, at one with the world, and only then living, living in the full sense of the word. All other times, and they may be good, bad or indifferent, I am not myself but another—

L'autre! Many others. There's no harm in it, to be sure. It may not be in the least injurious to the psyche or the immortal soul or what have you. But it's in these rare moments that I know that I know, that I feel complete and realized, that I am free of moods, fears and ambitions and above all, reach beyond happiness.

Art & Outrage

DETACHMENT

In Hermann Hesse's famous book *Siddhartha*, he has his hero say—"I can think, I can wait, and I can do without." To me these qualities make a man invincible. Especially, "to wait and to do without." America knows neither the one nor the other. Perhaps that is why at the early age of 200 years she shows signs of falling apart.

Sextet

In my own short life I've experienced the two tidal impulses: I've known evolution and involution, and stalemate and paralysis, and despair and ecstasy. What I thought was courage I've seen later was cowardice, and vice versa. I've had to learn to distinguish between hope and desire, between prayer and communion. Every time I finish a book I realize that nothing is finished, that the book is not important but writing itself, and not even writing, but expression, which can be on any plane. When I speak of ceding everything to the enemy I am thinking not only of pride, possessions, place, prestige, but all the evidence of creation. I don't wish to be attached to anything I've created any more than to a home, a country, an idea, or a memory. The act was important, not the product of the act. To become more and more creative is to become more and more detached, free, flexible, alive. To become fully alive. To become fully alive, to burst with life, that is my goal. Anything which must be defended is a fetter, only arrests the flow. No situation can be ignominious if one is detached.

Hamlet Letters

I think when you suffer somewhere and you can't escape, you begin to accept the situation and then you find marvelous things in it. So in the midst of my poverty and suffering and all that, I really discovered Paris, and the true French spirit and everything. And got to love it. Of course that's a hard thing to understand—how can you enjoy being right down to the very bottom? And that's the most important thing that ever happened to me—

to be without anything, no crutch of any kind. Cut off completely from any help, and to have to find it every day, this help to live from day to day. This is a very good thing, you know. You suffer, sure. You're miserable. But it's so interesting, it's so fascinating, you're so thoroughly alive, when you do that. You're living then with your instincts like an animal, and that's a great thing for us overcivilized people. To know again how to live like a bird of prey or, you know, an animal, wolfing every meal; and begging, and being humiliated, accepting it, being pushed down and then bouncing back up again; each day is a miracle that you get through, do you see. This is a very wonderful thing.

This is Henry, Henry Miller from Brooklyn

DESTINY

Every man has his own destiny: The only imperative is to follow it, to accept it, no matter where it leads him.

The Wisdom of the Heart

I am now absolutely at one with my destiny and reconciled to anything which may happen. I haven't the slightest fear about the future because I have learned how to live in the present.

The Cosmological Eye

Every man is working out his destiny in his own way and nobody can be of help except by being kind, generous and patient.

Henry Miller on Writing

DEVOTION

We live in an age when art and the thing of the spirit come last. The truth still holds, however, that through dedication and devotion one achieves another kind of victory. I mean the ability to overcome one's problems, not meet them head on.

Big Sur and the
Oranges of Hieronymous Bosch

True strength lies in submission which permits one to dedicate his life, through devotion, to something beyond himself.

The Time of the Assassins

ETERNITY

... to make a voyage is only an idea, that there is nothing in life but voyage, voyage within voyage. And that death is not the last voyage but the beginning of a new voyage and nobody knows why or whither, but bon voyage just the same.

The Cosmological Eye

Death. It has become intriguing to me because in the past ten years I have become sharply aware that one day I am going to die. Till then I hardly ever thought about my own death. How do I feel about it? What do I think about it? Well, nobody knows anything about death! It's a complete blank. No one ever came back from the grave. I have such great, great faith in life that it's difficult for me to think of the absence of life. I regard death as a transition from one form of existence to another. There may be such a thing as reincarnation, but if so I don't think it is as people imagine. What we see is transformation. We don't see annihilation. One thing changes into another. I have no fears about death. Sometimes I even welcome it. I lie in bed sometimes, when I'm feeling very good, and say, "Now is the time to die. I feel beautiful, fulfilled. Let it come now. I'm ready for it." So I've gotten to live with it, like a companion in waiting. You remember that when St. Francis was dying, he said, "Brother Death, I forgot all about you. I must write a poem to Brother Death." What a wonderful way to die! That's a little bit how I feel about it.

My Life and Times

And the door opened. It was called death,

which always swung open, and I saw that there was no death, nor were there any judges or executioners save in our imagining.

Nexus

Death itself doesn't frighten me, because I don't believe it's the end. All my intuitive feelings are that this cannot be the only world. It's too damn short, too ugly and too meaningless. There's got to be something more to it. Otherwise we should all blow our brains out.

People Magazine

FORGIVENESS

… there can be no solution, no end to crime, no end to man's injustice to man except through the tedious and painful increase of understanding, sympathy and forbearance. In trying to fix the responsibility, in searching for the motive and the cause of crime, we sink into a bog from which there seems to be no possibility of extrication. All is illusion and delusion. There is no firm ground on which to stand. Crime and punishment are rooted in the very fibre of man's being. Even the lovers of justice—perhaps especially the lovers of justice—stand condemned before the higher tribunal of love and mercy.

Sextet

FREEDOM

The struggle of the human being to emanci-
pate himself, that is, to liberate himself from
the prison of his own making, that is for me
the supreme subject.

The Books in My Life

A few years ago I stumbled on Hesse's *Siddhartha*. Nothing since the *Tao Teh Ching* meant
so much to me. A short book, a simple book,
profound perhaps, but carrying with it the
smile of that old man from Pekin over my
doorway. The smile of "above the battle."
Overcoming the world. And thus finding it. For
we must not only be in it and above it, but of it
too. To love it for what it is—how difficult! And
yet it's the first, the only task. Evade it, and you
are lost. Lose yourself in it and you are free.

Art & Outrage

Only where strict bodily discipline is
observed, for the purpose of union or communion with God, has the subject of sex
ever been faced squarely. Those who have
achieved emancipation by this route have,
of course, not only liberated themselves
from the tyranny of sex but from all other
tyrannies of the flesh.

Remember to Remember

For genius is, after all, the ability to deliver oneself from the circumstances in which one is enmeshed, the ability to free oneself from the vicious circle.

The Books in My Life

HEALING

Everybody becomes a healer the moment he forgets about himself.

Sexus

I know what the great cure is: it is to give up, to relinquish, to surrender, so that our little hearts may beat in unison with the great heart of the world.

The Colossus of Maroussi

If it weren't for the constant struggle on the part of a few creative types to expand the sense of reality in man, the world would literally die out. We are not kept alive by legislators and militarists...We are kept alive by men of faith, men of vision.

The Air-Conditioned Nightmare

HOME

"Home" is a condition, a state of mind. I was ever in revolt against places and conditions of being. But when I discovered "to be

at home" was like being with God, the
dread which had attached itself to the word
fell away.

The Books in My Life

I regard the entire world as my home. I
inhabit the earth, not a particular portion of
it labeled America, France, Germany, Russia…I owe allegiance to mankind, not to a
particular country, race or people. I answer
to God, not to the Chief Executive, whoever
he may happen to be. I am here on earth to
work out my own private destiny. My destiny is linked with that of every other living
creature inhabiting this planet—perhaps
with those on other planets, too, who
knows? I refuse to jeopardize my destiny by
regarding life within narrow rules which are
laid down to circumscribe it. I dissent from
the current view of things, as regards murder, as regards religion, as regards society, as
regards our well-being. I will try to live my
life in accordance with the vision I have of
things eternal. I say "Peace to you all" and if
you don't find it, it's because you haven't
looked for it.

Letter from Henry Miller to Trygve Hirsch

HUMILITY

… the forces which make the world are not null and void. The forces of life are working all the time, silently, underneath. We are all part of those forces; what the humblest man does also counts. And what one does not do counts too! In some cases counts heavily.

Hamlet Letters

I not only do my own marketing but I cook my own food, wash my own dishes and scrub my own floor—I handle my own garbage. There are people who pretend they have more important things to do, they couldn't be bothered with all these menial tasks. I find, on the contrary, it is no bother at all, in truth it is refreshing, stimulating, illuminating to perform these drudging tasks. How often, in handling the garbage have I received the most illuminating flashes! How often in washing the greasy dishes or cleaning out the sink have I meditated well and profitably! I might say in all seriousness that I am often nearer to God when doing the dirty chores than when listening to Bach or Mozart. So many writers seem to imagine that in order to write a good or a beautiful book they should refrain as much as possible from coming in contact with the

sordid, the mean, the ugly things of life. They think that to turn their back on evil is to put themselves face to face with the good.
Hamlet Letters

INDIVIDUALITY

The genius, whether through works or by personal example, seems ever to be blazing the truth that each one is a law unto himself, and the way to fulfillment is through recognition and realization that we are each and all unique.
The World of Sex

I see that no matter what stage of evolution or devolution, no matter what the conditions, the climate, the weather, no matter whether there be peace or war, ignorance or culture, idolatry or spirituality, there is only and always the struggle of the individual, his triumph or defeat, his emancipation or enslavement, his liberation or liquidation. This struggle, whose nature is cosmic, defies all analysis, whether scientific, metaphysical, religious or historical.
The World of Sex

Let each one turn his gaze inward and regard himself with awe and wonder, with mystery and reverence; let each one promulgate his own laws, his own theories; let each one work his own influence, his own havoc, his own miracles. Let each one as an individual, assume the roles of artist, healer, prophet, priest, king, warrior, saint.

The Cosmological Eye

We should not try to imitate him [Thoreau] but to surpass him. Each one of us has a totally different life to lead. We should not strive to become like Thoreau, or even like Jesus Christ, but to become what we are in truth and in essence. That is the message of every great individual and the whole meaning of being an individual. To be anything less is to move nearer to nullity.

Stand Still Like the Hummingbird

Tonight I would like to think of one man, a lone individual, a man without name or country, a man whom I respect because he has absolutely nothing in common with you. Myself. Tonight I shall meditate upon that which I am.

Black Spring

INNER LIGHT

But the last wall to give way is the wall which hems the ego in. Who reads not with the eyes of the Self reads not at all. The inner eye pierces all walls, deciphers all scripts, transforms all "messages." It is not a reading or appraising eye, but an informing eye. It does not receive light from without, it sheds light. Light and joy. Through light and joy is the world opened up, revealed for what it is: ineffable beauty, unending creation.

The Books in My Life

Light is not a manifestation of some physical law but one of the infinite aspects of spirit itself. And there is no light on earth which matches the inner light.

Art & Outrage

He [Abe Rattner] is painting the light which shines through the darkness, the light in the soul of man, which, no matter how deep the fall, remains inextinguishable.

Remember to Remember

LIFE ROLES

Whoever the Creator may be, one feels that He is not concerned with success or failure, sorrow or joy, but with the drama itself. It is up to each of us to discover the rules of the game. The problems that arise in the course of one's life are never really solved; they were not meant to be. The murderer had a different role to play than the saint; all that is asked is that one play his part the best he can. For the author of the play is really one's own self. ("I and the Father are one.") And so it is not the happy ending or the bad ending that matters, but the endless transmutation of which we are witness and prime mover at one and the same time.

The Paintings of Henry Miller:
Paint As You Like and Die Happy

I am a man who's constantly falling in love. People say I am an incurable romantic. Perhaps I am. In any case I'm grateful to the powers that be that I am that way. It's brought me sorrow *and* joy; I wouldn't want it any other way. People work better, create better, when they are in love. For it's true that if you are creative there is a lot of work involved. I often think of the Old Testament—and how God created the world in six days and then He found it good and He stopped. Supposedly He was satisfied with his creation.

But to me that is not an accurate picture of creation, because creation goes on continually; once you have begun you are part and parcel of your own creation and you cannot stop. All of us who have some awareness and some intelligence know that we have to play a role in life. I don't say we *elect* our role; maybe we were forced into it. But we do find ourselves playing a role. People often say, "Oh I can do this, or I could do that," but it's not true. There is no choice. You are what you are and you will be what you are. But this business of having a role to play, whether it's a humble one or a big one, doesn't matter; it gives traction to the ego, gives meaning to your life. You are fulfilled if you play your role to the best of your ability. The tragedy of our world is that people are not aware of their role, have no consciousness of it. They are to be pitied.

My Life and Times

LOVE

Love is the only protection; all other kinds of protection lead to war.

Stand Still Like the Hummingbird

Love is the drama of completion, of unification. Personal and boundless, it leads to deliverance from the tyranny of the ego.

The World of Sex

I can imagine a world—because it has always existed!—in which man and beast choose to live in peace and harmony, a world transformed each day through the magic of love, a world free of death. It is not a dream.

The World of Sex

Love is complete and utter surrender. That's a big word, surrender. It doesn't mean letting people walk all over you, take advantage of you. It's when we surrender control, let go of our egos, that all the love in the world is there waiting for us. Love is not a game, it's a state of being.

Reflections

In the realm of love all things are possible. To the devout lover nothing is impossible. For him or her the important thing is—*to love*. Such individuals do not fall in love, they simply love. They do not ask to possess but to be possessed, possessed by love. When, as is sometimes the case, this love becomes universal, including man, beast, stone, even vermin, one begins to wonder if love may not be something which we ordinary mortals know but faintly.

Sextet

… what the world of suffering millions demand, though they know not how to voice it, is not the elimination of injustice nor even the establishment of justice, but the satisfaction of a hunger more imperious still, because it is a positive and permanent need of the human heart. This is nothing less than the condition of love. Whoever is denied his rightful share of love is crippled and thwarted in the very roots of his being.

Sextet

MASTERS

The ability to revere others, not necessarily to follow in their footsteps, seems most important to me. To have a master is even more important. The question is how and where to find one. Usually he is right in our midst, but we fail to recognize him. On the other hand I have discovered that one can learn more from a child very often than from an accredited teacher.

Sextet

METAPHYSICS

A hundred thousand years from now, when we shall have conquered space—whatever that may mean—we shall probably be communicating with the angels. That is to say, those among us who no longer place such emphasis upon the physical body, those who have learned to use their astral body. The men, in other words, who have discovered that all is Mind, that what we think is what we are and what we have is what we truly want. Even in that distant day there may still exist two worlds—the hell the world has always been and the world of free spirits who know that the world is of their own making.

Sextet

In Aesculapian times man was still a whole being. He could be reached through the spirit. Body and spirit were one. Metaphysics was the key, the can-opener of the soul. To-day not even the greatest analyst can restore to men what they have lost. Each year there ought to be a congress of physicians meeting at Epidauros. First the medicos should be cured! And this is the place for the cure. I would give them first a month of complete silence, of total relaxation. I would order them to stop thinking, stop talking. Stop theorizing. I would let the sun, the light, the heat, the stillness work its havoc. I would let them become slightly deranged by the weird solitude. I would order them to listen to the birds, or the tinkle of goat bells, or the rustle of leaves. I would make them sit in the huge theatre and meditate—not on disease and its prevention but on health which is every man's prerogative. I would forbid cigars, the heavy black cigars of the Freudian school, and above all books. I would recommend the cultivation of a state of supreme and blissful ignorance.

Sextet

I have always been very interested in the occult, because I cannot accept this world. I know there is another world behind it which is the real world. The occult embraces many domains, from the gift of prophecy to palmistry and the reading of tarot cards. I've had my palm read and it's unusual that the heart and the head lines run together—they shouldn't. Yet my heart and my head run together. Now, ah, what does it mean? I don't know. I'm as interested in the knowable as in the unknowable, which is infinite.

This is Henry, Henry Miller from Brooklyn

MINDFULNESS

My loyalty and admiration, or adoration rather, has been constant for the same men all through my life. Whitman, Emerson, Thoreau, Rabelais above all. I still think no one has had a larger, healthier view of man and his universe than Walt Whitman. And there was always Lao-Tse, even before I read him. He stands there at the back of one's head like the great ancestor old Adam— what's all the fuss about, take it easy, sit down, don't get quiet or get quiet, rather, don't think, think—and from him the line of Zen masters which I only got wise to from the Villa Seurat days on—When you walk, walk. When you sit, sit. But don't wobble.

This is Henry, Henry Miller from Brooklyn

Enjoy every moment. What difference does it make whether you accomplish it today, next week or next month. Take life as it comes.

Conversation with Ben Grauer

Music—you sound a note; that leads to the next note; one thing determines the next thing, do you see. And when you get down to it philosophically, as in Zen, the idea is to live from moment to moment. This move decides the next step. You shouldn't be five steps ahead, only the very next one. If you keep to that you're always alright. But most people are thinking too far ahead, and out into sidelines. Think only what is right there, what is right under your nose to do. It's such a simple thing—that's why people can't do it.

This is Henry, Henry Miller from Brooklyn

MYSTERY

No matter what you touch and you wish to know about, you end up in a sea of mystery. You see there's no beginning or end, you can go back as far as you want, forward as far as you want, but you never got to it, it's like the essence, isn't that right, it remains. This is the greatest damn thing about the universe. That we can know so much, recognize so much, dissect, do everything, and we can't grasp it. And it's meant to be that way, do y'know. And there's where our reverence should come in. Before everything, the littlest thing as well as the greatest. The tiniest, the horseshit, as well as the angels, do y'know what I mean. It's all mystery. All impenetrable, as it were, right?

This is Henry, Henry Miller from Brooklyn

PASSION

To be always ecstatic. Be filled with a divine intoxication.

Conversation with Ben Grauer

When each thing is lived through to the end there is no death and no regrets, neither is there a false springtime; each moment lived pushes open a greater, wider horizon from which there is no escape save living.

Black Spring

Every day men are squelching their instincts, their desires, their impulses, their intuitions. One has to get out of the fucking machine he is trapped in and do what he wants to do. But we say no, I have a wife and children, I better not think of it. That is how we commit suicide every day. It would be better if a man did what he liked to do and failed than to become a successful nobody.

My Life and Times

PEACE

Peace is not the opposite of war any more than death is the opposite of life. The poverty of language, which is to say the poverty of man's imagination or the poverty of his inner life, has created an ambivalence which is absolutely false. I am talking about the peace which passeth understanding. There is no other kind. The peace which most of us know is merely a cessation of hostilities, a truce, an interregnum, a lull, a respite, which is negative. The peace of the heart is positive and invincible, demanding no conditions, requiring no protection. It just is. If it is a victory, it is a peculiar one because it is based entirely on surrender, a voluntary surrender to be sure.

The Colossus of Maroussi

To live for one another in the absolute religious meaning of the phrase: we will have to become planetary citizens of the earth, connected with one another not by country, race, class, religion, profession or ideology, but by a common instinctive rhythm of the heart.

Remember to Remember

We must die as egos and be born again in the swarm, not separate and self-hypnotised, but individual and related.

Sexus

If there is to be any peace it will come about through being, not having.

The Wisdom of the Heart

What man wants is peace in order that he may live. Defeating our neighbor doesn't give peace any more than curing cancer brings health. Man doesn't begin to live through triumphing over his enemy nor does he begin to acquire health through endless cures. The joy of life comes through peace, which is not static but dynamic. No man can really say that he knows what joy is until he has experienced peace. And without joy there is no life, even if you have a dozen cars, six butlers, a castle, a private chapel and a bomb-proof vault.

The Colossus of Maroussi

PSYCHE

I don't know the answers as to why people do this or that. I don't think one does anything deliberately or for reasons that are apparent. The things we do are for reasons far deeper than we pretend and much more obscure.

My Life and Times

PURSUIT OF TRUTH

Nothing is easier to make sport of than the yearning for the sublime.

The Books in My Life

But to return for one moment to the master-disciple business. Each of us is both at once, is he not? The only master is life. To be just a master is to be static, dead. As long as we are alive, we are growing, stretching out our hands toward God...any God. And God is reaching down to us. No end, no conclusion, no completion. Perpetual becoming.

Art & Outrage

How I love the dying words of St. Thomas Aquinas: "All that I have written now seems so much straw!" Finally he saw. At the very last minute. He knew—and he was word-less. If it takes ninety-nine years to attain such a moment, fine! We are all bound up with the Creator in the process. The ninety-eight years are so much sticks of wood to kindle the fire. It's the fire that counts.

Art & Outrage

We are all born searching for heaven. We can define it in many ways: outer space, human worthiness, enlightenment, and so on. The search for higher realms, the outer limits, as it were, is the strongest and most vital impulse of all.

Reflections

SAVIORS OF THE WORLD

For me the only true revolutionaries are the inspirers and activators, figures like Jesus, Lao-Tse, Gautama the Buddha, Akhenaton, Ramakrishna, Krishnamurti. The yardstick I employ is life: how men stand in relation to life. Not whether they succeeded in overthrowing a government, a social order, a religious form, a moral code, a system of education, an economic tyranny. Rather, how did they affect life itself. For, what distinguishes the men I have in mind is that they did not impose their authority on man; on the contrary, they sought to destroy authority. Their aim and purpose was to open up life, to make man hungry for life, to exalt life—and to refer all questions back to life. They exhorted man to realize that he had all freedom in himself, that he was not to concern himself with the fate of the world (which is not his problem) but to solve his own individual problem, which is a question of liberation, nothing else.

The Books in My Life

The figures who have most influenced the world all practiced detachment: I mean men like Lao-Tse, Guatama the Buddha, Jesus the Christ, St. Francis of Assisi and such like. They did not remove themselves from the world, nor did they deny life; what they did was to lift themselves out of the vicious circle of every day life which leads nowhere, unless to confusion, sorrow and death. They reaffirmed the spiritual values of life. None of

them advocated war to uphold their beliefs.
Remember to Remember

At no time in the history of man has the world been so full of pain and anguish. Here and there, however, we meet with individuals who are untouched, unsullied, by the common grief. They are not heartless individuals, far from it. They are emancipated beings. For them the world is not what it seems to us. They see with other eyes. We say of them that they have died to the world. They live in the moment, fully, and the radiance which emanates from them is a perpetual song of joy.
The Smile at the Foot of the Ladder

It's been said that we will never have another savior. There have been enough saviors. They have all shown man the way. Now man must save himself.
My Life and Times

SERVICE

The one desire which grows more and more is to give. The very real sense of power and wealth which this entails is also somewhat frightening—because the logic of it seems too utterly simple. It is not until I look about

me and realize that the vast majority of my
fellow-men are desperately trying to hold
on to what they possess or to increase their
possessions that I begin to understand that
the wisdom of giving is not so simple as it
seems. Giving and receiving are at the bottom one thing, dependent upon whether
one lives open or closed. Living openly one
becomes a medium, a transmitter; living
thus, as a river, one experiences life to the
full, flows along with the current of life, and
dies in order to live again as an ocean.

The Colossus of Maroussi

Serve life and you will be sustained.

Big Sur and the
Oranges of Hieronymous Bosch

Life is servitude. One is voluntary servitude
and one is involuntary. The voluntary servitude takes in the really great figures like a
St. Francis. He elects to dedicate himself to a
life of service to humanity.

Conversation with Ben Grauer

The only ones who can truly affect the
world and the destinies of man are those
who are completely dedicated to sacrifice,
because they have emancipated themselves,
lived out their personal problems, found

true anonymity and realized that there is nothing beyond giving. They want nothing and expect nothing. For all lesser individuals sacrifice is only a lesson, an expiation, a purgation, etc. It is to their own interest not for the benefit of others. For the former it has no terrors, nor can it deplete them. They have learned, as it were, the secret of harnessing themselves to the inexhaustible power which governs the universe.

A Literate Passion

SOLITUDE

In Athens I experienced the joy of solitude; in New York I have always felt lonely. The loneliness of the caged animal, which brings on crime, sex, alcohol and other madness.

The Colossus of Maroussi

No man is alone who is thoroughly himself.

Hamlet Letters

All my life I had this faculty of meeting people, of studying them, of being part of them. It matters little from what class they came, what education they had, and so on. Fundamentally all are alike. Yet each one is unique. Strange paradox. All are reachable—and redeemable. Those in prison are often better than those who put them there. Thieves and pimps are far more interesting than preachers and teachers—or most psychologists. Nobody should be wholly despised. Some should be murdered perhaps, in cold blood. But not all murderers are murderers at heart. I have often wondered how many people I have met in my long life. I know for certain that during the four and a half years I spent in the Western Union I met and talked to a good hundred thousand. And yet I regard myself as a loner. I don't mind being alone. As I said somewhere else—"At the worst I am with God!"

Book of Friends: A Trilogy

SOUL

Always we are led back to the heart. It is there that everything is determined. A community must be organized around the heart, otherwise, no matter how rational the theory, how stout the principle, it will fall apart. This is the true theatre of operation: the heart. What happens outside in the world, as they say, is only the echo of the passion play which goes on in the soul of every individual.

Remember to Remember

Before it is possible to love one another, as we are so often enjoined, it is necessary to respect one another, respect the privacy of the soul.

Stand Still Like the Hummingbird

SPIRIT

What good are words if the Spirit behind them is absent.

The Air-Conditioned Nightmare

I'm a religious man but not a religionist. Let's put it very simply. When we say that "man does not live by bread alone," that's a symbolic statement tersely put. What it means is that it isn't his success in the struggle for life—his getting bread, getting security, protecting wife and children—that sustains and supports him. It's something you can't put your finger on, it's spirit. You can't name it, can't define it. It's greater than everything else; it includes everything.

My Life and Times

I always like to use the word "acceptance." It's a very big word for me. Accepting life as it is, seeing what it is, and taking it for what it is, not having illusions and delusions about it. When I got rid of my "idealism" that was a big step, I would say, toward health. In Rabelais' "Gargantua" there is inscribed over the portal of the Abbaya de Thélème, "Faites ce que voudras!" "Do as you please!" in other words. St. Augustine put it another way. He said, "Love God and do as you please." How wonderful! It means that spirit, the Holy Spirit, is important—not morals, not ethics. If one is imbued with the right spirit one can't do wrong. Then to do as one pleases can only bring happiness.

My Life and Times

SPIRITUAL LIFE

There are two things in life which it seems to me all men want and very few ever get (because both of them belong to the domain of the spiritual) and they are health and freedom. The druggist, the doctor, the surgeon are all powerless to give health; money, power, security, authority do not give freedom. Education can never provide wisdom, nor churches religion, nor wealth happiness nor security peace.

The Air-Conditioned Nightmare

If we have not found heaven within, it is a certainty we will not find it without.

The Books in My Life

More and more people are discovering the euphoric effects of spiritualism. Everyday I see ads in the newspapers for lectures, workshops, gurus—everything imaginable for spiritual growth and enlightenment. That's America for you. In order to earn the rights to a more fulfilled existence, we have to be willing to spend money. The Americans have to make money on everything, including enlightenment. None of those groups or gurus are giving anything away for free, at least I don't know of any.

As long as Americans are hungering for enlightenment, there will be people who are ready to exploit those needs...

The most sensible of all the enlightened men, Krishnamurti, said, "Don't put your faith in anyone, you have it all inside you. You're always asking the masters, why don't you ask yourselves? Forget the masters."

As a final word, I'd say that until you know yourself, no amount of searching or seeking will bring you closer to God. God is within you. You don't have to pay someone to tell you that, I say it because I know it's true.

Reflections

The mastery of great things comes with the doing of trifles; the little voyage is for the timid soul just as formidable as the big voyage is for the great one. Voyages are accomplished inwardly, and the most hazardous ones, needless to say, are made without moving from the spot.

The Colossus of Maroussi

Do not put the Buddha (or the Christ) beyond, outside yourself. Recognize him in yourself.

Stand Still Like the Hummingbird

But if I should happen back this way once more, if given the choice, I'd like not to live the life of the artist, or the writer. I'd like more than anything, to be a man who grows flowers. It seems to me that the life of the horticulturist is the cleanest, the purest, the most natural life of all. The man who tends a garden is the man most directly in touch with God.

Reflections

SURRENDER

Why not accept the challenge of the Spirit and yield? Why not surrender, and thus enter into a new life?

The Time of the Assassins

When God answers Job cosmologically it is to remind man that he is only a part of creation, that it is his duty to put himself in accord with it or perish. When man puts his head out of the stream of life he becomes self-conscious. And with self-consciousness comes arrest, fixation, symbolized so vividly by the myth of Narcissus.

The Books in My Life

Joy is like a river: it flows ceaselessly. It seems to me that this is the message which the clown is trying to convey to us, that we should participate through ceaseless flow and movement, that we should not stop to reflect, compare, analyze, possess, but flow on and through, endlessly.

The Smile at the Foot of the Ladder

One needs either a heaven or a hell in which to flourish—until one arrives at that Paradise of his own creation, that middle realm which is not a bread-and-butter Utopia of which the masses dream but an interstellar realm in which one rolls along his orbit with sublime indifference.

Henry Miller on Writing

TRUST

The key word is trust. Trust everything that happens in life, even those experiences that cause pain, will serve to better you in the end. It's easy to lose the inner vision, the greater truths, in the face of tragedy. There really is no such thing as suffering simply for the sake of suffering. Along with developing a basic trust in the rhyme and reason of life itself, I advise you to trust your intuition. It is a far better guide in the long run than your intellect.

Reflections

TRUTH

Meaningful acts require no stir. When things are going to wrack and ruin the most purposeful act may be to sit still. The individual who succeeds in realizing and expressing the truth which is in him may be said to have performed an act more potent than the destruction of an empire. It is not always necessary, moreover, to mouth the truth. Though the world crumble and dissolve, truth abides.

The World of Sex

... I do feel that truth is linked to violence. Truth is the naked sword; it cuts clean through. And what is it we are fighting, who love truth so much? The lie of the world. A perpetual lie.

Art & Outrage

UNIVERSE

The law of the universe dictates that peace and harmony can only be won by inner struggle. The little man does not want to pay the price for that kind of peace and harmony; he wants it ready-made, like a suit of manufactured clothes.

The Time of the Assassins

The universe is run by laws, if you break the law you have to pay the penalty. That's only fair, isn't it? Besides how are you going to learn except through experience?

Mother China and the World Beyond

For his autobiographical sketch for "Americans Abroad" (1932), Miller wrote: "Born N.Y. City, 1891. No schooling. Was tailor, personnel manager in large corporation, ranchman in California, newspaper man, hobo and wanderer. Was a 6-day bike racer, concert pianist, and in my spare time I practiced sainthood. Came to Paris to study vice."

Henry Valentine Miller
(December 26, 1891—June 7, 1980)

When Henry Miller came into the world the Victorian Age had another ten years to go and writers of the day tiptoed around four-letter words. As a lad in Brooklyn where his father ran a tailor shop, he was dressed in a Lord Fauntleroy suit with lace collar and lived a sheltered life as the darling of his parents. He took piano lessons, became an exuberant bike rider and developed a passion for the cinema. And, of course, he became a zealous reader, finding inspiration in such diverse writers as Whitman, Balzac, Conrad, Dostoyevsky, Haggard and Madame Blavatsky.

Generally speaking, the first half of his life was an unhappy bungle. He had a number of dreary clerical jobs, including one with the Western Union, an ill-fated first marriage to an older woman, Beatrice Wickens, and a writing career that seemed to be going nowhere. In spite of the odds, an irrepressible zest heated inside him to the boiling point. He had always been a natural storyteller, a great listener and made friends easily. Unlike the dull and boorish "Henry" portrayed in the film *Henry and June*, the real Henry radiated an infectious charm. Even when he was down and out he was a man of humor, refinement and tact. "Always merry and bright," became his motto.

He married again, to the woman who both inspired and degraded him, the notorious June Mansfield. They broke out of the American coffin and fled to Paris, Miller was reborn, living on ten francs a day and writing what became his first and most important book, *Tropic of Cancer*, published when he was 43 and immediately banned in all English-speaking countries. The book's opening words: "I have no money, no resources, no hopes. I am the happiest man alive. A year ago, six months ago, I thought that I was an artist. I no longer think about it, I am."

From that time on, books poured forth. *Cancer* was followed by *Black Spring*, *Tropic of Capricorn* and *The Rosy Crucifixion*, constituting his autobiographical romances, along with *The World of Sex* and *Quiet Days of Clichy*. At the same time, under the tutelage of Emil Schnellock, he developed a passion for painting in watercolor, which endured to the end of his days and inspired his book *To Paint Is to Love Again*.

During his expatriate years in Paris he established lifelong friendships with Anais Nin, Lawrence Durrell, Blaise Cendrars and

Alfred Perles. He also became a prodigious letter-writer, resulting in volumes of correspondence with Nin, Durrell, Michael Fraenkel and Perles and later with Wallace Fowlie, Brenda Venus and Hoki Tokuda, his fifth and last wife.

The outbreak of World War II forced Miller back to America after a stay in Greece, where he wrote what many consider his most profound book, *The Colossus of Maroussi*.

Once back in his homeland he met with Abraham Rattner. They acquired an old car and embarked on an odyssey to rediscover America, as described in *The Air-Conditioned Nightmare*, *Sunday After the War* and other essays.

Now in his fifties, Miller felt the need to settle down. He acquired a small house in California's remote coastal mountains of Big Sur, atop Partington Ridge. Without telephone or electricity, with his back to America and facing the East with a photograph of a smiling Tibetan above his dining table, he lived with his new wife, Lepska, and fathered two children, Valentine and Tony. Here he wrote *Big Sur and the Oranges of Hieronymous Bosch* and *The Books in My Life*, soaked in the sulfur baths of Esalen and made lasting friendships with Emil White, Ephraim Doner, Walker Winslow, Harrydick

Ross, Maud Oakes, Bill Webb and many more.

It took the Supreme Court, in 1964, to declare the sale of *Tropic of Cancer* constitutional, bringing Miller into official respectability at last. As Karl Shapiro wrote in the introduction to the Grove Press edition of *Cancer*, "Miller is probably the only author in history who writes about such things [erotica] with complete ease and naturalness. Lawrence never quite rid himself of his puritanical salaciousness, nor Joyce; both had too much religion in their veins."

By 1963 Miller, now in his seventies, found himself alone again, his marriage to Lepska then Eve McClure ended, and the Big Sur life too rigorous. He moved into a bourgeois neighborhood of Pacific Palisades with the help of Lepska and her new husband, Robert Warren. From the outside, the house was one of those pseudo-Colonial creations with white pillars and a front lawn. Inside, it was all Miller, with his wildly impressionistic watercolors all over the walls and a Ping-Pong table in the living room. Here, he lived out his days, never allowing himself not to be in love. He was the same age as Goethe had been when he fell in love with a nineteen-year-old girl.

Miller had a crush on a Chinese movie

actress named Lisa Lu and then a Japanese popular singer known as Hoki Tokuda, who favored miniskirts over kimonos. She, at twenty-seven, became his last wife. It lasted scarcely two years, during which time he wrote *Insomnia or the Devil at Large* and began *The Book of Friends* trilogy.

Circulatory problems plagued him and he suffered a mild stroke. He posted on his front door this notice drawn from Hermann Hesse: "When a man has reached old age and has fulfilled his mission, he has a right to confront the idea of death in peace. He has no need of other men, he knows them already and has seen enough of them. What he needs is peace. It is not seemly to seek out such a man, plague him with chatter, and make him suffer banalities. One should pass by the door of his house as if no one lives there."

During these last years, he continued to write, paint watercolors using the Ping-Pong table as an easel and enjoyed the fond caretaking of dear friends like Twinka Thiebaud and Bill Pickerill. He maintained his correspondence with a hundred friends and fell in love one last time, with Brenda Venus, an actress who drove a hundred miles every Wednesday night to take him to dinner at his favorite Chinese restaurant in Hollywood. Miller lived for those outings with keen spirits. Surely those romantic dinners extended his life by several years.

Henry Miller died softly in the arms of his housekeeper, Bill Pickerill, in June 1980, a few days before the first copies of *The World of Lawrence*, a treatise which he wrote in the thirties and had eagerly awaited publication, arrived at his doorstep. There was never anyone like him, either as an author or a man.

—NOEL YOUNG
publisher, Capra Press

Acknowledgments

BLAIR FIELDING has lived near the Gaza Strip in Israel, worked with a travel agency in London, and lived in an Appalachian cabin. She is a licensed psychotherapist specializing in grief and loss issues and midlife transitions. Fielding is a co-founder of *ElderWise* and presents *Age Power* workshops across the country.

Index